Hawk Eyes

written by J.L.W

Tellwell Talent

www.tellwell.ca

ISBN

978-0-2288-0638-7 (Hardcover)

978-0-2288-0639-4 (Paperback)

This story is dedicated to the teachers in my life:

Beth, Nancy, Mother Nature, and especially my children.

Thank you for the perspective!

Every morning, Lulu bounces from bed with the first whisper of dawn. Lulu loves mornings.

There are always things to discover, fun to be had, and joy to soak up.

But today, Lulu does not feel like getting up early.
She is not excited about this morning.

Lulu's mom is away for work. She left when Lulu was
sleeping, and she is not coming home until tomorrow.

That means an entire day and bedtime
without Mom. This makes Lulu sad.

Lulu loves her dad time, but Dad is home every day. Weekends are special because Mom and Dad are both home. But today is Saturday, and Lulu's mom is away.

"Maybe I will just stay in bed today," thinks Lulu, feeling a little sorry for herself.

"Luluuuu," comes Dad's voice as he climbs the stairs.

Lulu can hear her dad coming, along with the pitter-patter
of four furry paws and panting breath.

"The sun is up. It's a new day. I wonder what magic is coming our
way?" sings Dad. Lulu's dad loves turning sentences into songs.

Suddenly, the door springs open. Aunt B bounds into
the room, jumps onto Lulu's bed and starts giving Lulu
morning kisses. Lulu loves waking up to Aunt B's kisses.

"Wake up sleepy head. It's time to get out of bed," sings Dad. "Why don't we take Aunt B to the park?"

"Without Mom?" asks Lulu, trying not to giggle as Aunt B stops her kisses and tilts her head at the word "park."

"Sure," says Dad. "We can make it a great day, and maybe Aunt B can have some ice cream."

Lulu pulls the covers up tight over her head.
She wants her mom to be there too.

"I know it is not ideal Lulu, but lots of moms and dads travel for work. Let's find a positive perspective."

"What does per-spec-tive mean?" Lulu asks, peeking out from under her covers and scrunching her nose.

"Perspective is a big word that means we each get to choose how we look at something," says Dad. "And how we look at something can change how we feel about it."

"What do you mean?" asks Lulu.

"Well," says Dad, "let's look at today two different ways. We can stay home and be sad, or we can take Aunt B to the park and enjoy this gorgeous day. Then, before we know it, Mom will be home."

Lulu thinks about what her dad is saying.
She does want to have fun today. "Would you like
that Aunt B?" Lulu asks her loving pup.

"Aunt B says, 'Yes'!" Lulu tells her dad, as she
slides from her bed, trying to leave her
gloomy feelings behind.

Lulu's local park is perfect. It has the best jungle gym, a big fountain, Shelly's Sundae Shack, and lots of grassy hills where Aunt B can run free.

Lulu also loves lying on the hills and watching the clouds float by. "That one looks like Aunt B," laughs Lulu.

"I think it looks like a llama," says Dad. "I guess we see it from different perspectives."

"Look at that hawk flying way up there," Dad points out. "What do you think she is doing? What do you think she sees?"

"I'm not sure," says Lulu. "What do you think she sees from way up there Aunt B?"

After a moment, Lulu adds, "Aunt B says the hawk can see everything from up there."

"She sure can," agrees Dad. "She is definitely seeing much more than we can see from down here. Maybe we can learn from her.

"I can only see from down here," says Lulu, scrunching her nose in thought.

"Well, the hawk can see far and wide from way up high," explains Dad. "We can try to do that too. When we look at any moment in a different way, it can change how we feel. That's perspective, Lulu."

"I sort of understand," says Lulu.

"When we looked at the clouds, we saw different things, you saw Aunt B, and I saw a llama. If we looked at the whole sky what would we see? Lots of animals? Lots of clouds in the blue sky? We can choose to look at a small piece or at a bigger picture and that can change what we see, and maybe what we feel."

"This morning, when you were missing Mom, how did you feel?" asks Dad. "Sad," says Lulu.

"Did we have a great afternoon?" Dad asks.

"The best," laughs Lulu.

"We decided to make today a fun day, even though you were feeling sad. Like our friend the hawk, you looked further. You looked further than your sad feelings and you saw a bigger picture. You found a positive perspective," explains Dad.

"And we had a great day," says Lulu.

"Yes," says Dad. "You looked at the day from a different perspective and had fun. Great job, Lulu."

Lulu smiles. She imagines herself on the hawk's
back, soaring up high in the sky.

She can see the whole town. There is her house, her school, the
entire park, the arena where she plays hockey, and way far away,
is mom, finishing up her work, getting ready to come home.

Lulu giggles. "Thank you for the new perspective, Hawk."

At bedtime, as Lulu's Dad tucks her into bed with his
usual, "It's time for bed, sleepy head," Lulu smiles.

Mom is going to be home soon.

Lulu can't wait to tell her mom about the fun day they all had.

And thanks to Dad and her hawk friend, Lulu also
knows the next time Mom travels it will be okay.
Lulu will look at the bigger picture and see things
from a different, more positive perspective.

CPSIA information can be obtained
at www.ICGtesting.com
Printed in the USA
LVHW070050150120
643683LV00025B/138

9 780228 806387

Peaceful Piggy Bedtime

Wisdom Publications
199 Elm Street
Somerville, MA 02144 USA
wisdomexperience.org

Library of Congress Cataloging-in-Publication Data is available.
LCCN 2019058092

ISBN 978-1-61429-674-4   ebook ISBN 978-1-61429-675-1

24 23 22 21 20
5 4 3 2 1

Designed by Katrina Damkoehler. Cover art by Kerry Lee MacLean.

Printed on acid-free paper that meets the guidelines for
permanence and durability of the Production Guidelines for
Book Longevity of the Council on Library Resources.

Printed in Korea.

PEACEFUL PIGGY BEDTIME

Story by **Sophie Maclaren**

Illustrations by **Kerry Lee MacLean**

Wisdom

It's time to go to sleep.
Some friends are sleepy, and some are not.
Some are already nodding off

—and some want to bounce around.

Now it's time to go from busy to peaceful.
These mindful bedtime exercises will help us
have a good night's sleep.

Now lie down and close your eyes.

Take three nice big breaths.

Feel your breath going in and out . . .

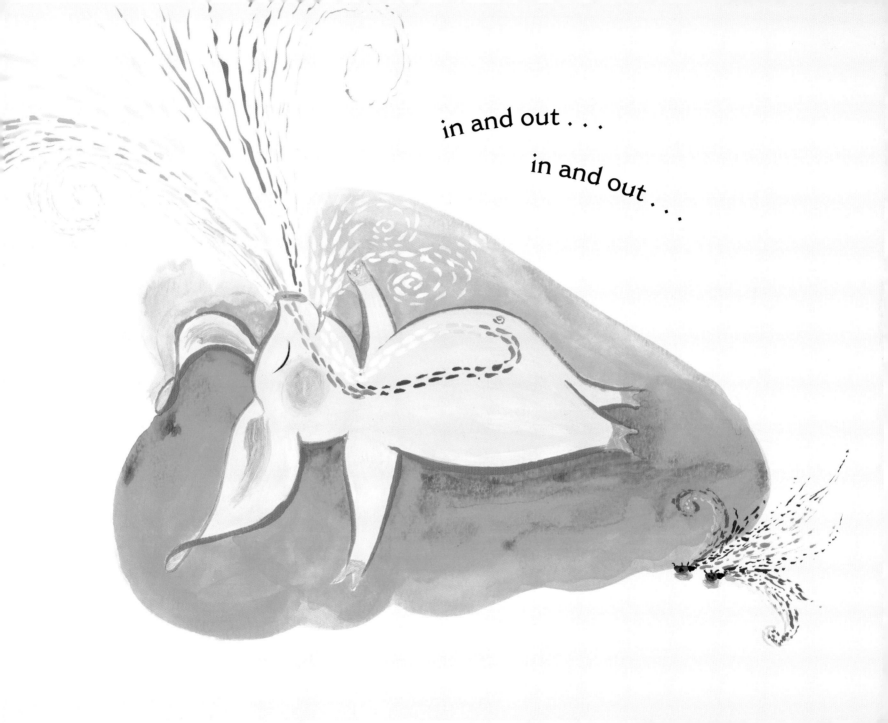

in and out . . .

in and out . . .

APPRECIATION

Think about what you did today.

What was one thing you really liked about today?

"Playing with my puppy, Poppy!"

KINDNESS

How was someone kind to you today?

How were you kind to someone today?

"Here you go."

"Yummy, thanks!"

HELPING

How did you help someone today?

How did someone help you today?

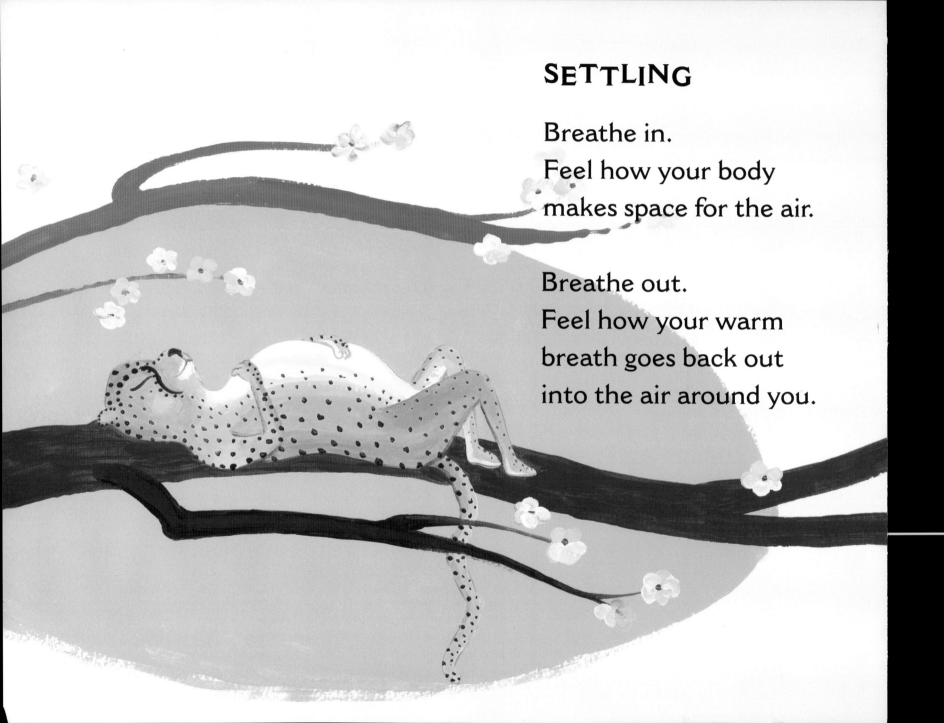

SETTLING

Breathe in.
Feel how your body
makes space for the air.

Breathe out.
Feel how your warm
breath goes back out
into the air around you.

breathe in, breathe out . . .

breathe in, breathe out . . .

breathe in, breathe out . . .

FEELING

Lift up one leg.
Stretch it out as far as you can,
and a little farther.
Wiggle your toes.

Then let that leg drop back on to the bed,
rock it from side to side and let it be.

Do the same with your other leg.

Lift up your chest and tummy.
Reach as high as you can,
and a little higher.

Wiggle your belly.
Then drop back on to the bed,
rock from side to side,
then let it be.

Lift up your hips.
Lift them as high as you can,
and a little higher.

Wiggle your hips.
Let them drop to the bed,
rock them from side to side,
then let them be.

Lift up one arm.
Stretch it out as far as you can,
and a little more.

Wiggle your fingers.
Then let the arm drop onto the bed,
rock it from side to side
and let it be.

Do the same with the other arm.

And if you have a tail,
wiggle and relax that too!

Lift up your head a little.

Stretch your neck a tiny bit.

Softly let your head
drop onto your pillow,

then rock your head
from side to side
and let it be.

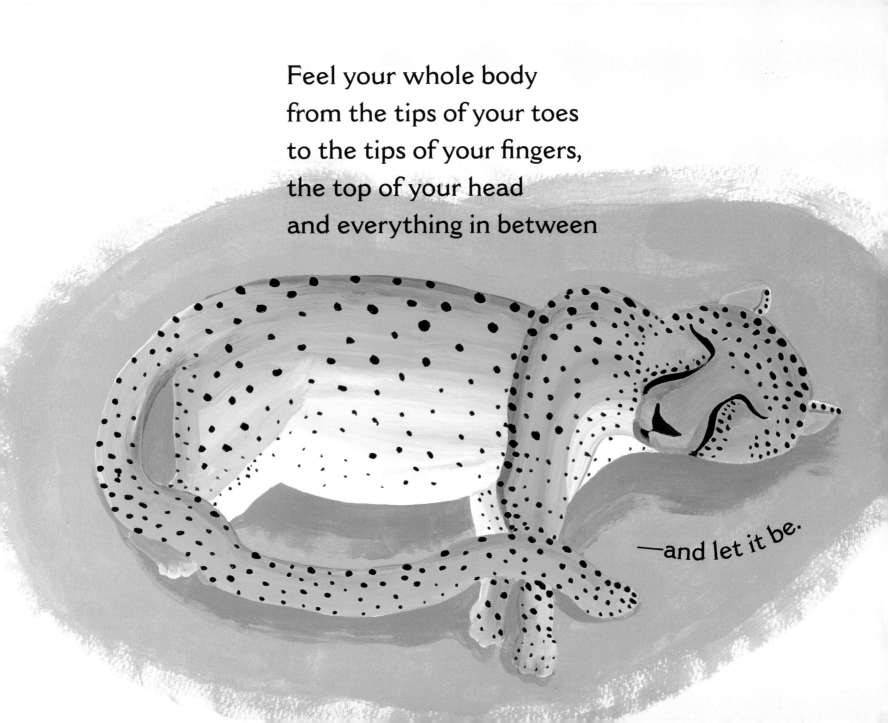

Feel your whole body
from the tips of your toes
to the tips of your fingers,
the top of your head
and everything in between

—and let it be.

BELLY BREATHING

Take a big, B I G breath,
in through your nose and
all the way down to your tummy.
Feel how your belly gets bigger,
making room for all the breath.

Let your tummy soften,
and push the air back up through your chest
and out your mouth
letting it disappear back into the air around you.

Your tummy gets bigger and smaller
like waves in the water
with your breath coming and going.
Now your body is ready for sleep.

Let's get your mind ready for some peaceful dreams.

LOVING

Put one hand on your chest and feel the warmth of your heart.

When you feel settled, think about someone you love, someone in your family, a pet, a friend . . .

or someone you know is having a hard time.

Imagine what they look like when they are really happy.

What makes them happy?

Make a wish for them to be happy.

Put that wish inside a balloon and
float it all the way to them.

The balloon pops,
the happy little wish
goes into their heart

and they smile.

FRIENDS WITH YOURSELF

Put your hand over your heart.
Feel the air moving your belly bigger and smaller
like waves in the water.

Feel the warmth of your heart.
Say something loving to yourself before falling asleep,
like, "I like you! Have sweet dreams!"

In dreams and in life
you can be your own best friend.

DREAM MEDITATION

Get all snuggled up on your side or your back
—however you like to fall asleep.

Close your eyes and imagine a peaceful little
candle flame, glowing warm in your heart.

Watch as it gently flickers and bobs up and down,
the way candle flames do.

Just keep watching it shining so peacefully.

Watch the flame . . .

breathe in, breathe out . . .

breathe in, breathe out . . .

watch the flame . . .

breathe in, breathe out . . .

watch the flame . . .

. . . sweet dreams.

Dear Parents,

Peaceful Piggy Bedtime is the encapsulation of my own experiences as a child, practicing mindfulness with my mother, Kerry Lee MacLean, who is the author of *Peaceful Piggy Meditation* and *Moody Cow Meditates*. It also grows from my experiences as a mindfulness student, teacher, and researcher working with people of all ages around the world. We recommend taking the time to try all the exercises one time, and then, if you like, you can pick one or two from each category each night.

Bedtime can be a joy; a quiet time, a nice cuddle—a sleepy angel. Bedtime can also be a challenge; riled energy, hidden anxieties—a restless little monster! This book is intended to provide children with an effective bedtime ritual to relax the body, warm the heart, settle the mind, and drift into a peaceful sleep. Parents may find they sleep better, too!

Thousands of studies in the last decade have shown the wide range of benefits of a daily mindfulness practice to our mental, physical, emotional and social well-being. Many of these factors are the precursors to a good night's sleep. As researchers begin to understand how essential quality sleep is to our health and well-being in a multitude of ways—and how few of us are getting it—it makes sense to establish a mindful bedtime routine to prepare for the best sleep.

Clear transitions in our day are important for children and adults—they enable us to consciously switch gears to engage fully in each new task and activity throughout our day. For a parent this could be transitions from emails, to meetings, to family time, to sleep—all of which require us to switch gears to be present in different ways. If we are mindful of these transitions, we can allow a moment where we mentally close one task in order to fully and skillfully engage in the next. Without these conscious pauses our lives can begin to feel a bit like a novel with no punctuation marks—a blur of overlapping, never-ending activities and experiences, and when it comes to bedtime the day is a blur, the body is tired, and our minds are still racing, keeping us awake. The same is true for our children.

There are two things you can do earlier in the day in anticipation of a peaceful bedtime. First, ensure the physical space is conducive to the mind settling down. Our minds are easily stimulated, so the less distraction, temptation, and chaos around, the better. Remove all electronic devices like mobile phones and tablets, and any clutter and toys, particularly from around the bed. If there's a television set or computer that can't be easily removed, cover it with something like a scarf or a pillowcase. And, second, make sure your child has had an opportunity to talk about any stressful situations they may have faced at home or in school at least an hour before bedtime. This way, negative emotions and thoughts have been processed and let go of by the time bedtime comes around, helping your child to be relaxed and ready for the family's mindful bedtime routine.

Most of us are mentally stronger in the morning, whereas bedtime is more vulnerable. We can acknowledge this vulnerability and transition time by following a predictable bedtime ritual in which our children feel safely held and can relax.

The opening reflective exercises help children revisit the goodness in their day, thus cultivating a sense of gratitude and positivity which leads to a feeling of well-being. The breathing practices soothe the nervous system, helping the body and mind to slow down and relax. The final dream exercise clears and soothes the mind, ushering the whole family into a truly peaceful sleep.

Peaceful dreams!

SOPHIE MACLAREN

Dedicated to Josh Bartok, my editor and friend, who has proven himself time and again to be a genuine peaceful piggy. And to my grandchildren: Colin, the love-dove of peace; Lucy Bee, kindness incarnate; and Eloise, an artful soul who quietly creates harmony everywhere she goes.

—KERRY LEE MACLEAN

Dedicated to my father, Hamish Maclaren, and mother and stepfather, Kerry and Hector MacLean, whose deep dedication to mindfulness and compassion both as practitioners and teachers has inspired me since childhood. —SOPHIE MACLAREN

ABOUT THE AUTHOR AND ARTIST

SOPHIE MACLAREN is a mindfulness trainer and consultant specializing in mindful leadership, workplace well-being, and mindfulness for families. Sophie leads mindfulness courses at Oxford University and is the founder of Estia Wellspace, a mindfulness and well-being center in Oxford, England. She had an early introduction to mindfulness from her parents and began assisting her mother, Kerry Lee MacLean, with teaching her pioneering mindfulness programs for children when she was nine years old. Since then she has been leading mindful arts, yoga, and meditation programs, as well as mindful business and leadership trainings internationally for two decades.

KERRY LEE MACLEAN has dedicated her life to starting a worldwide family meditation movement. She is the author of ten books, including *Peaceful Piggy Meditation*, *Moody Cow Meditates*, and *The Family Meditation Book*—an expanded edition of which is in the works. Kerry is Sophie's mom, and together they have happily led mindful arts, meditation, and yoga programs for children, teens, young adults, and their parents internationally since 1989.